For Mishti, Robene and Sanjee - HB

For Sushila, Terry and Sue - RJ

First published in
Great Britain in 2004 by
Chrysalis Children's Books

Published in 2004 by Sterling Publishing Co., Inc.
387 Park Avenue South, New York, NY 10016
Text copyright © 2004 Henriette Barkow
Illustration copyright © 2004 Richard Johnson
Distributed in Canada by Sterling Publishing
c/o Canadian Manda Group,
165 Dufferin Street,
Toronto, Ontario, Canada M6K 3H6

10 9 8 7 6 5 4 3 2

Designed by Sarah Goodwin

Printed in China

ISBN: 1-4027-1756-3

If Elephants Wore Pants...

Henriette Barkow

Illustrated by
Richard Johnson

Sterling Publishing Co., Inc.
New York

Last night I had trouble falling asleep, so I tried counting elephants instead of sheep. An elephant came and took me by the hand, and whisked me away to Elephant Land.

Out in the yard, we skipped in the sun,
wearing fluffy pink pants
and having great fun.

We walked to the woods to visit the bears. Elephant wore brown velvet pants, just like theirs.

The circus was next and I cheered from the stands, as he juggled and balanced in bright rainbow pants.

Out in the orchard in pants of pear green,
the elephant hid and could hardly be seen.

We saw pants—and some undies!—
hung out to dry, as we whizzed in an
airplane way up in the sky.

On a cold frosty night we tried to see Mars, and the elephant's pants were covered in stars.

Dancing with fireworks over our heads, Elephant's pants were a sparkling red.

We drove to the coast to breathe the sea air, with some bright golden pants and the wind in our hair.

We drove for a while and
then stopped at the store,

where the elephants buy
these fun pants they adore.

And then one last stop—a parade!— but by then I was starting to feel very sleepy again. So I closed my eyes in my soft, comfy bed, and had elephant dreams swirl around in my head.